A Scottish Duke for Christmas

CHAPTER ONE

London, April 1789

Dear Reader,

Your intrepid correspondent has it on good authority that a certain duke, with lands north of the Scottish border, has had the unfortunate luck to be jilted by his lady love. Rumor also has it that the lady in question, the eldest daughter of a lesser nobleman has done a moonlight flit and fled London to be with a secret lover. The ballrooms of London society are said to be agog with the news...

Ewan Radley, Duke of Strathmore, screwed up the scandal sheet and threw it headlong into the fireplace. He watched as the flames hungrily consumed it.

He didn't need to read anymore. All that mattered was that the rest of London's elite now knew the scandalous secret he had kept hidden for the past month.

Lady Beatrice Hastings had called off their engagement and disappeared. His life was in complete disarray.

'I'll be the laughing stock of the *ton*,' he muttered.

In drawing rooms and at breakfast tables in the very best homes in London, he would be the main topic of discussion this morning.

By rights, he shouldn't care. It wasn't as if theirs had been a love match. Lady Beatrice was the eldest daughter of an old family friend. Of fine bloodlines and burdened with a substantial dowry, she had been the perfect candidate for the position of his duchess. She and of course her younger sister, Caroline.

Events were still too recent for him to fully comprehend, but he sensed that at some point soon the full extent of the damage caused by his rash decision to bed Beatrice, would be laid bare before him.

He pushed his breakfast plate away, food offered no comfort to the cold pit of his stomach.

'Shall I have your carriage brought around your Grace?' asked his butler.

The House of Lords was sitting that day. As Duke of Strathmore, Ewan had responsibilities that even a scandal such as this could not hold at bay.

'Yes, Hargreaves. Let us get out into the maelstrom as soon as we can,' he replied.

With the House of Lords soon to rise for the Easter break, he only had a week in which he would have to maintain a low profile. Once Parliament was in recess, he could escape London and seek refuge at his castle in Scotland.

And knowing London society as he did, by the time he returned, yet another scandal would have taken the place of his in the public mind.

CHAPTER TWO

London, November 1789

Lady Caroline Hastings sat and stared at her cold toast.

At the other end of the table her parents, Lord and Lady Hastings, were having their daily discussion.

The Beatrice Briefing, she had privately dubbed it. Every morning for the past eight months, her father had received a daily briefing from his agents as to the search for her older sister.

'The lead in Newquay had turned into another dead end,' Lord Hasting remarked.

His wife closed her eyes before letting out a dejected sigh.

Caroline silently gave her mother her dues. Without fail, the countess left the house every day and went about her business as a leader of London's *ton*. Not once; since Beatrice's disappearance had she missed a single event or declined an expected invitation. She had maintained the stiff upper lip so valued by the elite class.

No one but the immediate Hastings family knew the truth. That, in the months following Beatrice's disappearance Lady Hastings had come close to a full emotional breakdown. But, fighter that she was, she had managed to keep her tears and pain private.

Caroline excused herself from the table and headed into the hallway intent on retiring to her room. Her fervent hope being that her mother did not expect Caroline to accompany her to any social gatherings this day. She did not need another day of having to endure the spiteful whispers at social gatherings wagering as to whether the wild nature of the eldest Hastings daughter would someday surface within the younger one.

It hadn't taken long for acquaintances, and then disappointingly, friends to begin avoiding her company. No one wanted to be associated with an unmarried young woman who had a *fallen* sister.

It wasn't the first, nor she expected, the last time that her sister would make life more than a little difficult for Caroline.

As she reached the bottom of the staircase which led to the second floor of the elegant townhouse, there was a loud knock at the front door.

Caroline stopped and waited. It was most unusual for anyone to call this early in the morning unless it was a matter of grave urgency.

Her breath caught in her lungs as she saw the Duke of Strathmore cross the threshold and hand the family butler his hat and cane.

The man Caroline had loved and once thought she would marry. The man her sister had stolen from under her nose.

Ewan Radley was still as handsome a man as he had been the first time she set eyes on him some five years earlier. His dark brown hair having been ruffled by his hat, stood up in places. Ewan, being a man not given to vanity, made no effort to bring it under control.

While the butler went into the breakfast room in search of his master, Ewan waited in the foyer.

Caroline indulged in a private study of her sister's former fiancé. The man she had long loved from afar.

A soft smile crept across her lips as she watched him pick a piece of lint from his long black greatcoat. He rolled it between his long fingers.

Fingers she had once dreamed would touch her naked skin. Caress and stroke her as Ewan taught her the pleasures of the flesh.

'Lady Caroline.'

She blinked away the sensual dream and composed herself before taking an uncertain step toward him.

'Your Grace, how good to see you. I trust that you are well?'

Ewan dipped into a gracious bow as Caroline reached his side. She offered him her hand, making every effort to still the tremble which always threatened to overcome her whenever he was close.

'I am well, thank you for asking. I have come to see your father,' he replied.

The door behind her opened and her father stepped out into the hall.

'Strathmore. I take it you have a purpose in visiting at this unsociable hour?'

Caroline swallowed down a protest at her father's curt behavior. The Duke of Strathmore had been a short-lived beacon of hope for the earl in finding someone to tame his reckless eldest daughter. The loss of hope had been hard for him to bear.

'My apologies for the early hour of my visit, but I have news which could not wait until a more civilized time, Ewan replied.'

He glanced at Caroline.

'Lord Hastings, is there somewhere that you and I could discuss matters in private?'

A grey pale appeared on her father's face. Caroline clenched her hands together as fear gripped her. Her father kept his gaze locked on Ewan.

'Caroline, go sit with your mother.'

Lord Hastings closed the door of his study behind him, and for a moment stood with his back to Ewan, head bowed.

When he did finally turn, there was a stiffness in his bearing. His shoulders were pulled back, his spine ramrod straight. He looked for all the world like a man about to receive a dozen lashes.

Pity threaten to overwhelm Ewan; Beatrice's father did not deserve the news he was about to receive. He forced a deep breath into his lungs and pulled a letter from out of his coat pocket.

'I received this earlier this morning. It came from Lady Beatrice's maid, by way of Manchester.'

Lord Hastings glanced down at the paper in Ewan's hand before looking away.

'A moment if you don't mind Strathmore. Let me savor the last moment before you confirm my darkest fears. Because at this juncture I still have two daughters. I suspect, however, that is a fact, which is shortly to be irrevocably changed.'

Ewan stood silent, remembering that he too had experienced a similar feeling only an hour or so earlier.

'Is she dead?'

Their gazes met once more before Ewan nodded his head.

Lord Hastings staggered to the nearest chair and slumped down into it. He covered his eyes with a trembling hand and wept. Ewan took a seat in the chair opposite and quietly waited.

'This will be the death of my wife. She has only managed to maintain her sanity up to this point because she has been holding onto the fervent hope that Beatrice would come to her senses and walk back through our front door. Lord knows what will become of my family now,' said Lord Hastings.

Ewan unfolded the letter.

'There is more.'

Several minutes later, Lord Hastings sat back in his chair. His hands gripped the leather arms.

'A child you say?'

'Yes, a child she died giving birth to some two weeks ago. The blackguard she ran away to be with, abandoned her when he discovered she was with child,' Ewan replied.

'But why? If he loved her why did he abandon her? I don't understand,' Lord Hastings replied.

This was the moment Ewan had been dreading. His role in the death of Beatrice.

'Because the child is mine.'

CHAPTER FOUR

'Thank you for undertaking the journey to Manchester, Caroline. I know it must be hard for you having just lost your sister.'

Caroline gave Ewan a controlled smile. She didn't have the heart to tell him the truth.

That she had tried to mourn her sister. Even managed to shed a genuine tear or two. But that had been her limit. Any sisterly affection between the Hastings sisters had died long ago.

The best she could manage was to keep up appearances for the sake of her parents. Her mother was busy following all the socially accepted conventions of mourning. While Beatrice had pointedly refused to follow society's rules during her life, Lady Hastings was at pains to ensure that at least in death her daughter would adhere to social expectations.

Black curtains in the windows and reeds laid out in the street in the front of the townhouse to soften the sound of passing horses hooves gave ceremony to the process of grief. Structure and rules brought comfort to Lady Hastings.

Lord Hastings, in turn, had turned to stone. Locked within his own grief, he simply went through the motions of life.

'Mama felt it best that I come. A female member of the family should be present to assist with the babe,' she replied.

What her mother had in fact instructed Caroline to do, was to get out of London for the foreseeable future. This new scandal surrounding her sister threatened to derail any hope the Hastings had to see Caroline properly settled into a society marriage. Once word got out that a bastard child was now in the frame, society matrons would be gently steering their eligible sons in the direction of other more suitable girls.

'Forget spending any more time in London this year my dear. Go to Manchester with your father and then retire to Hastings Hall until he has to return to the House of Lords in January. You and I shall stay out of society until the beginning of the Season in May.'

Only when the Season's balls and parties began would Caroline know the true extent of the damage to her marital prospects.

She shifted on the hard leather seat of the carriage and tried to stretch the stiffness out of her back and shoulders. A pang of guilt added to her worries. It was wrong to think of herself at such a time. Beatrice, for all her many faults, was dead. And somewhere in a boarding house in Manchester a motherless child now lay waiting for someone to claim him.

'We shall stop at Loughborough to change the horses. You will be able to take a walk and get some fresh air,' said Ewan.

As he sat in his seat opposite and looked out the window, Caroline noticed a sadness about Ewan she had not noted earlier in their long journey north. Until this moment, she hadn't tried to think how difficult this terrible turn of events must be for the duke. That he too may be suffering.

She had once thought she knew Ewan's mind, but that foolish notion had been dashed when, to her heart's dismay, he had chosen Beatrice over her.

An uncomfortable thought entered her mind. What if he had truly loved her sister; and was now facing the awful truth that his dreams of winning Beatrice back to his side were gone forever? Her parents may not be the only ones lost in the depths of grief.

It was time to offer a piece of socially acceptable pity, an olive branch of sorts.

'I am sorry for the heartache you must be feeling Lord Strathmore, this must be a very difficult time for you. I do hope your son is able to give you some consolation for the loss of your beloved,' she offered.

The words had barely left her lips before she was regretting them. Ewan looked across at Lord Hastings who was fast asleep in the carriage next to Caroline.

'She was not my beloved. I think you and I can share that

much honesty with one another. I let myself be dazzled by Beatrice's magic and sexual charms. Our marriage would have been a travesty of the institution.

Your sister had at least the decency to throw me over for someone she loved. She could very well have married me and then made me a cuckold,' he replied.

He was calm, but Caroline caught the bitterness of his words. He had been a fool and they had all paid dearly for it.

Lord Hastings stirred in his sleep and the jolt of the carriage hitting a rut in the road brought him awake.

Caroline and Ewan exchanged a look of understanding. The conversation was at an end.

They reached Manchester mid-morning two days later.

Ewan offered to take Caroline to their hotel near the cathedral gates, but she refused.

'Beatrice was my sister; and therefore, I am this child's closest living female relative. I didn't come all this way to be set aside,' she said.

Her words cut through Ewan like a knife. Whether Caroline meant them as a criticism of him or not, they hit home. He *had* set her aside and chosen her sister. If she was bitter she had just cause.

Little over a year earlier he and Caroline had shared enough ballroom dances to have onlookers commenting on what a handsome couple they made. He had invited the whole family to his private box at the Theatre Royal and sat next to Caroline all evening during the opera. London society had begun to buzz with rumors of an expected engagement announcement.

And then Beatrice had turned the full heat of her sexual presence on him and he had been lost. Caroline had every reason to hate both Beatrice and himself. Her sister had stolen what by rights should have been hers, and he had been complicit in the extreme.

Watching as she climbed down from the carriage and stood in the cool northern air adjusting her skirts, Ewan knew he would never be able to tell her just how truly sorry he was.

How much he regretted letting his lust dictate his future. He should have followed his heart and married Caroline. She would never know how much he still loved her.

'This is the address?'

He looked to Lord Hastings who was pointing toward a narrow alleyway which led off the main street.

'Yes, number twenty-three,' Ewan replied.

Number twenty-three Blackbird Lane was a thin grey stone building which towered some three floors up. The front of the boarding house hung somewhat drunkenly out by several feet into the street. Ewan hazarded a guess that it dated from somewhere around the fourteenth century.

The street itself stank of a heady mixture of horse manure and dead fish. Ewan couldn't think of a more wretched place for Beatrice to have spent her final days. The sooner he retrieved their child, the better.

On the third level of the boarding house, they stopped at a badly battered door.

Ewan knocked.

He was about to knock for the third time when the door opened and a young woman's face appeared. She looked from Ewan to the Hastings.

'Thank the Lord,' she muttered.

All three of the traveling party stepped into the boarding house room. Apart from a small bed, and a table with two chairs there was no other furniture. A ragged green curtain covered the single window. No sunlight warmed the room.

'I take it you are the ladies maid who wrote to me. If so, I've come about the baby,' Ewan announced.

The maid's eyes grew wide with fear.

'Shhh. I've only just managed to get him to sleep,' she replied.

She pointed to a tiny lump wrapped up in a shawl laying on the bed.

Caroline rushed past both of them and went to the bed. For a moment she stood silent, staring at the bundle, before bending down and gently picking it up.

The bundle made a squeak and the maid whimpered.

Caroline turned to them and held up the bundle. Ewan caught first sight of his sleeping son.

All the anger and regret he had let boil inside for the past months instantly dissipated. Here was a defenseless child. An innocent in this whole domestic disaster. He was a father and this child was now his responsibility.

'Hannah, you have done magnificently. How can we ever thank you enough?' said Caroline.

Hannah burst promptly into tears. Lord Hastings finally stirred from his emotional stupor and stepping forward, put a comforting arm around her.

'It will be alright soon young miss. We shall have you and the baby home at Hastings Hall and away from this place,' he said.

Ewan held his tongue. Now was not the time to argue over the future of the infant. Caroline meanwhile was cooing gently to the baby she held in her arms. Her natural mothering instincts evident.

'Did his mother give him a name?'

Hannah shook her head.

'No. Lady Beatrice passed away not long after she birthed him. I took to calling him David because he looks like my cousin David.'

David. Scotland had been ruled by kings named David. It fit well with being the son of a duke. Ewan approved of Hannah's choice.

It was fitting and just, that the woman who had seen the boy through the dangerous early days of his life, should be the one to name him.

'Then David it is,' said Ewan.

CHAPTER SIX

The rest of their short stay in Manchester was spent arranging a suitable headstone for Beatrice's at present unmarked grave. At some point, her body would be exhumed and removed to Hastings Hall in Kent where it would be interred in the family crypt.

Caroline and Hannah went to the local drapers and bought some basic baby clothes, blankets, and a warm travel shawl. By day's end, they had quit the boarding house and taken up residence at the hotel.

David cried on and off all day, fraying Caroline's nerves. Hannah, she noticed, seemed to have developed the ability to ignore the infant's constant crying.

After returning to the hotel, Caroline and Hannah went up to the room they were to share. Hannah ordered a jug of fresh milk and a spoon from the hotel kitchen.

'So, this is how you have had to feed him this whole time?' Caroline asked as she watched Hannah patiently attempt to feed David. She knew enough about babies to know that women of her class often employed the services of a wet nurse. Hannah had made no mention of such a woman.

'I got a wet nurse for the first few days, but when she discovered that he had been born out of wedlock, she wanted more money. I realized I would run out of money very quickly if I did that, so I started getting milk from a lady a few

streets over who has a cow in her garden. I've had to make do
with a bottle and spoon. He seems to like it, but it does take
a long time. He is constantly crying for food. I'm sure with a
wet nurse he would thrive.'

Caroline made a mental note to secure the services of a
wet nurse as soon as they reached Hastings Hall.

Now that David had been found and rescued. Caroline had
had time to consider the events of the past weeks in
Manchester. Beatrice had been dead for almost four weeks, yet
Hannah had only now written to Ewan and told him of the birth
of his son.

Things didn't make sense.

Once David had settled to sleep in the basket she had
purchased that afternoon, Caroline decided it was time to talk
to Hannah.

'Come let us sit, we should talk,' she said.

Hannah nodded. From the way she sat on the edge of the
chair, it was clear she had been waiting for this moment. Soon
she had revealed the whole tale of how Beatrice had fled
London in pursuit of a naval officer whom she had in mind to
marry.

'He told her she should go back to Lord Strathmore and
marry him. Then when she said no, he told her to have the baby
and give it up. Only then would he come for her,' said Hannah.

She began to cry.

'Lady Beatrice was so angry. She wanted to be rid of the

babe, so she took some poison hoping to kill it. Only, it made her very sick.'

A chill rippled through Caroline. Beatrice had tried to kill her own child rather than go back to Ewan and marry him. She reached out and took Hannah's hand.

'Then what happened?'

'When the officer discovered what she had done, he called a wicked, evil woman. He said he would never marry her. That she was eternally damned. We never saw him again.'

Hannah went to Beatrice's travel trunk which they had retrieved from the boarding house and opened it. She returned to Caroline bearing a letter in her hand.

'She wrote this a week before she died. Said I was to send it to Lord Strathmore if anything happened to her. She was very weak all through her confinement, the poison had hurt her and I think she knew she wouldn't survive the birth. Made me promise to send the babe to a foundling hospital. I even took him as far as the front door, but I couldn't do it. That's when I finally wrote to Lord Strathmore. Figured if he didn't want David, then I would bring him to your father.'

Caroline took the letter and placed it unopened into her travel bag. David was her priority, the letter from Beatrice could wait.

'Why didn't you just pack up things and bring David to London? My father would have taken you both in.'

Hannah put her hand into her skirt pocket and pulled out

a handful of coins.

'With the money that had to go to pay for Lady Beatrice's burial, I didn't have enough to buy a ticket back to London.'

Caroline's heart sunk. The poor girl had been left with barely any means to support herself and David.

'I did consider trying to sell what was left of Lady Beatrice's things, but there isn't much I could sell without running the risk of being arrested. Your sister sold most of her gowns and nice things in the past few months.'

Caroline rose from her seat and went to her sister's travel trunk. There were a few odd pieces of clothing, but all of Beatrice's fine gowns and silk slippers were gone.

At the bottom of the trunk, she spied a familiar blue velvet box. With heart racing, she opened it.

Inside was a beloved family heirloom, she had lost all hope of ever seeing it again.

The Hastings family pearl and gold tiara glistened in the light as she lifted it out of the box. Beatrice had held out to the very end and not sold the priceless piece of jewelry.

Hannah had been right not to try and sell the tiara. A lady's maid found in possession of such an item would likely be charged with theft and meet her end at the hands of the public executioner.

Caroline came and took hold of Hannah's hand.

'You have done so much for our family. I promise we shall take care of your every need from this day forward.'

'Now you have his blanket firmly wrapped, and his feet are covered up well. He doesn't like it when his toes get cold.'

She bent down and placed a tender kiss on David's forehead, before handing him over to the nursemaid.

The nursemaid Ewan had managed to secure in Manchester gave a huff of disgust.

'This isn't the first babe I have managed my lady, they are all the same. Treat them with a firm hand and they will soon learn who is in charge.'

With David held in her arms, the nursemaid climbed up into the Strathmore travel coach and closed the door behind her.

Standing alongside her father, Caroline watched as the various trunks and boxes were loaded up onto the top of the coach. Though she was physically present, she felt as if she was witnessing matters from a great distance. Lord Hastings had hold of her arm, but she felt no sensation. The expected tears did not threaten.

She was numb.

While she had been making plans and preparations to take David home to Hastings Hall, her father and Ewan had decided on another course of action. Ewan would exert full parental rights over his son and take him home to Scotland.

David Radley, as he was to be called would be raised by his father and treated the same as any other children Ewan Radley would sire in the future. While he would never be his father's heir, David would enjoy the full benefits of being the son of a duke.

Caroline's plan to become David's mother by proxy had been knocked sideways.

Soon Ewan and the last living trace of her sister would be gone. Fear spoke to her heart that it would be a long time before she saw either of them again.

Ewan stepped out from the hotel. He rubbed his hands together and nodded his head. Caroline knew enough of him to know that Ewan was in an apprehensive mood. He was about to embark on the journey of fatherhood with no wife.

'Strathmore, all set?' her father asked.

Ewan walked over to where Caroline and Lord Hastings stood. He shook hands with the earl.

'Thank you for all that you have done for me. I cannot begin to tell you how much I appreciate it. I know this is a difficult time for you and your family, and I admire you for having put your mourning to one side to assist in the safe retrieval of David. I shall not forget your kindness. Nor yours Lady Caroline.'

He offered her his hand. For a moment Caroline simply stared at Ewan's outstretched hand, unable to offer her own.

Take it. Say goodbye; and then let this all be at an end

for now.

'Godspeed your Grace. I hope the journey home is a good one,' she finally replied, offering him her gloved hand.

The crowded Manchester street provided her with the social limitations of not offering Ewan anything more than a mere handshake, and for that she was grateful. Ewan tipped the lid of his hat and scrambled aboard the coach.

Caroline stepped back and watched as the door emblazoned with the Strathmore family crest of a prancing horse over a set of three, four-pointed stars, closed behind him.

The driver flicked his whip over the horses and the coach pulled away from the side of the street. Within a matter of minutes, it had turned the corner and was lost from sight.

Caroline closed her eyes and gritted her teeth.

He was gone.

Lord Hastings squeezed her hand. 'Come, my dear, it's time we collected our things and made the journey home to Kent, there is nothing left here for us now.'

***

They had barely made it back to their hotel room before there was a loud rap on the door. As soon as Lord Hastings opened the door, Ewan strode inside.

In his arms, he held a wailing David. Both father and son were red-faced with rage.

'What?' Caroline stammered.

Ewan deposited David into her arms.

'The nurse slapped him the second he began to fuss. When she went to hit him a second time, I took her firmly by the throat. It goes without saying that her employment has been terminated,' he roared.

Caroline began to pace the room. She patted David's back, in an effort to calm the offended infant.

After what seemed like an eternity, David's cries of indignation eventually died down and softened into a pitiful sob. Caroline cooed gently in his ear and his tears finally ceased.

Ewan meanwhile, stood with his gloves in his hands, slapping them hard on the side of his leg, his gaze never once leaving her.

'I need Lady Caroline to accompany me to Scotland,' he finally announced.

'Yes.'

She didn't wait for her father to register his protest; her mind was made up in an instant. Lord Hastings could muster all the arguments he wished against her going unaccompanied to Scotland, but she was determined to go.

'What of your reputation? If London society discovers where you have gone and why you will be forever ruined,' said her father.

She came to his side. A now calm David still held in her arms.

'No one need ever know. We left London in secret. If anyone asks, you can tell them that I am in mourning at Hastings Hall. Besides, Papa, I won't be gone all that long. I just need to see David settled at his new home, and then I shall return.'

Ewan picked up on the theme.

'My mother and Aunt Maude are in residence at Strathmore Castle. I am sure once they have taken David under their wing, Lady Caroline will be free to return home. At most it will be a matter of a few weeks,' he added.

The panic in his voice took her by surprise. Ewan was normally a man in control of his emotions, or at least outwardly so. To see him otherwise, gave her pause.

Her father reached down and ran his fingertips through the brush of dark hair on David's head. It was exactly the same shade as Beatrice's. As he withdrew his hand, it was shaking.

'This goes against all my better judgment. But, as you are both clearly set on this course, I doubt there is little I could say at this moment to change either of your minds. My grandson's wellbeing is what is paramount here, and as such I shall acquiesce to your request. But Caroline must travel incognito, and she must take the maid Hannah with her.'

Ewan's hands dropped to his sides.

'Agreed. Thank you, Lord Hastings. I promise I shall do everything in my power to protect Lady Caroline and her reputation. The last thing I would ever wish to do would be to cause more distress to your family.'

* * *

A little over an hour later, Ewan joined Caroline, David and the maid Hannah on board the Strathmore coach. Ewan sat back in his seat and looked out the window. He dared not meet anyone's gaze until they were well clear of the city.

It had been a bold move and he was still a little in shock that he had managed to pull it off. Against all hope, he had both his son and Caroline on board the coach and they were now headed for Strathmore Castle in Scotland.

The extent of his plan did not reach any further at this point, he simply knew he needed Caroline to be with him. Nothing more. Only when the coach finally made it out onto the Great North Road, did Ewan allow himself to relax. As the horses' heads turned northward, toward Scotland, he began to formulate a plan.

CHAPTER EIGHT

Fortunately for the traveling party, David spent a great deal of the five-day journey northward fast asleep. With Caroline, Hannah and occasionally Ewan holding him, he was content. Unfortunately for Caroline, he rarely fully settled with the others, so she was left to shoulder the bulk of the workload.

She was fast gaining an understanding and appreciation of the toll that being a new mother had on a woman. While she had been spared the nine months of pregnancy and then childbirth, she still found herself exhausted by days end. How women got up from the labor of birth and then looked after a family was something she found unfathomable.

A good night's sleep at Strathmore Castle was top of her list for journey's end.

A few hours outside of Falkirk, Scotland the coach departed from the Great North Road and onto a side road. Ewan took a sleeping David from a grateful Caroline and wrapped his tiny son up in his arms.

'Get some sleep, we shall be at the castle before nightfall. You will need to be somewhat refreshed when you meet with my mother and Aunt Maude. I expect they will have one or two questions for the both of us,' he said.

Caroline accepted his offer without hesitation. She was bone weary and after five long days in the coach, her back was stiff and sore. She pulled her woolen blanket up around her shoulders and closed her eyes. She would deal with the Dowager Duchess of Strathmore and Aunt Maude when the time came.

When she finally awoke several hours later, she was greeted by the sight of Ewan holding his infant son up to the window of the travel coach.

'There it is my wee laddie. Home.'

Caroline sat up in her seat and pressed her face to the glass.

Out of the coach window, she caught her first glimpse of Strathmore Castle.

A towering Norman era structure loomed large over the landscape and the village below. It wasn't the elegant gothic style castle of lower England that Caroline had seen during her lifetime. Rather, this heavy stone behemoth had been built to withstand attack from a large army. Its dense walls looked nigh on impenetrable.

'It's huge,' she muttered.

Ewan looked over at her and smiled.

'Never been taken. Has withstood countless attacks and sieges for over five hundred years,' he replied. The pride in his voice evident at his family's long-held achievement.

She looked at David, with his tiny fingers wrapped around his father's small finger. Sadness pierced her heart. David Radley would never hold ownership of the castle of his father and forebears. He would forever, be a footnote in the castle's long history. A natural born son, never able to inherit either title or castle. She could only hope that Ewan Radley would do everything in his power to give his first born all the advantages that could be afforded to him. Son of a duke and grandson of an earl, yet David Radley was still tainted as a bastard, and nothing could change that fact.

After passing through the small village which sat in the shadow of Strathmore Castle, the travel coach crossed over the castle's heavy wooden drawbridge and through the gateway. The coach entered the courtyard and drew to a halt in front of the main steps of the keep.

As the coach drew to a halt, a group of servants quickly surrounded it. Caroline made to rise from her seat, but Ewan held out his hand.

'Wait,' he said.

'The Defender of Strathmore is returned!' came the shout from the assembled castle servants. Ewan smiled and opened the door. A chorus of cheers and applause erupted throughout the castle courtyard.

He climbed out of the coach and disappeared into the throng of well-wishers.

Hannah seated next to Caroline, clapped her hands and laughed.

'What a welcome home!'

Caroline caught the mood and beamed. She had never seen anything like it. Little wonder the castle had held firm all those years. The men and women of the castle truly loved their lord.

Ewan soon returned.

'Come,' he said.

He held out his hand and helped Caroline down from the coach.

At the sight of Caroline, a collective gasp rippled through the crowd. A nearby servant bowed low as she walked past him. Out of the corner of her eye, she caught sight of a smiling Ewan shaking his head. He held up his hand, in a gesture which she took to mean *not yet.*

A blush of red raced to her cheeks. She wasn't used to being the center of attention, let alone having crowds of cheering people gathered around her. She looked urgently for Ewan.

She was intent on taking David from his arms and thus allowing Ewan to greet his steward and staff properly. She was worried about the baby amidst the milling crowd.

Her searching eyes found him. He was kneeling on the lowest of the steps of the castle keep, his son held aloft in an almost feudal supplication. The image of a knight kneeling, holding his sword before his king entered her mind. A medieval tableau laid out before her.

Standing on the third step, hands clasped together, was Lady Alison, the Dowager Duchess of Strathmore. Caroline had met her several times over the years; most recently at

Strathmore House in London when Beatrice and Ewan's betrothal had been announced. Lady Alison had a fearsome reputation as a woman who did suffer fools gladly.

The Dowager Duchess was clad in a simple blue gown, with a Strathmore tartan shawl draped over her shoulders to keep the chill winds at bay. Her gaze was firmly fixed on the infant held aloft before her.

Several steps to the right of her was a middle-aged woman, clad in black, with a tartan sash across her chest. Caroline guessed that she must be Aunt Maude.

Lady Alison stepped forward and took David lovingly into her arms. But the instant she held him, David let out an almighty wail.

Ewan got swiftly to his feet as the knightly tableau cracked. Caroline started forward, but before she could reach the steps, Aunt Maude lifted David from out of his grandmother's hands and placed him over her shoulder.

The crying stopped immediately.

'Maude, working your magic again I see,' said Lady Alison. She left David with his great aunt and came to Caroline's side.

She gave Caroline a tender kiss on the cheek. 'I am so very sorry for your loss my dear. You are a welcome guest here at the castle.'

'Thank you. This was an unplanned visit. Ewan asked that I come to make certain that David arrived safely at his father's ancestral home. My father agreed to my coming.'

Lady Alison raised an eyebrow.

'Yes of course. Come in and we shall have a room prepared at once for you.'

CHAPTER NINE

There was no avoiding the inevitable conversation, so Ewan sought out his mother as soon as he knew Caroline had been settled in her room.

'Where do I begin,' Ewan said, as he put his head around the door of his mother's sitting room.

The Dowager Duchess of Strathmore was alone.

Lady Alison rose from her chair and came to her son, embracing him in a long motherly hug.

'Maude has gone to the village in search of a wet-nurse. In the meantime, the maid Hannah has said they can manage with cow's milk.'

Aunt Maude the first and last bastion of pragmatism. Always thinking of the practical side of things. Not one for fancy clothes or exotic food. For Maude, the story of David; and how he had come to be at Strathmore Castle could wait. The babe needed feeding.

'I received your letter yesterday, so I understand that

David is Beatrice's child and that she is dead. Poor girl, what a horrid end.

What I don't understand is why Lady Caroline is here. And why the devil Lord Hastings let her travel here with you, accompanied only by a maid. You have already ruined one of his daughters, and yet he willingly offered up the second one. Has the man gone mad?'

Ewan considered his reply. The clear and obvious reason was that David had taken to his aunt, and Ewan's sanity would not have survived the journey to Scotland if he had been forced to share the travel coach with a screaming infant.

The other possible reason for bringing Caroline with him was still coalescing in his mind. Was Caroline the one for him; and could she meet his soul deep hunger for a passionate and love-filled union?

Even if she was, he wasn't entirely certain that he had the power to overcome both current circumstance and past wrongs to make her his duchess.

'David fussed as soon as he was away from her. Lord Hastings, allowed Caroline to accompany us to Scotland,' Ewan replied.

Lady Alison frowned.

They both knew that for an unmarried woman of Caroline's standing to be in the company of a man not of her family, was inviting scandalous gossip of the worst kind. If London society knew she had traveled with Ewan to Scotland, her chances of any sort of suitable match would be dashed.

'We made certain that no one saw her on the journey here. She and the maid Hannah were always careful to keep the hoods of their cloaks covered when we arrived at the coaching inns along the way. No one knows she is here.'

Lady Alison closed her eyes and sighed.

'I know she is here and so does Maude. I don't think you have thought through the full consequences of Caroline being under your roof my lad.'

His mother's disapproval stung more than it should. She was right. Yet again he had gone off and done something without thinking it through. His impetuous nature had got him into this situation in the first place, and all that he was doing now, was likely to make it worse.

'As soon as things are settled here; and David has become accustomed to his home, I shall make suitable arrangements to send her home to Kent,' he replied.

Lady Alison took hold of his hand.

'Can I give you some motherly advice?'

'Pray do,' he replied, knowing he had no choice but to listen.

'Think about why you really brought Caroline north to Scotland with you. I think in time you may find that the truth is more than just a crying infant.'

'If I do, you shall be one of the first to know,' he replied.

CHAPTER TEN

Strathmore Castle was the perfect place to take David. Scotland was far enough away from the prying eyes of London society for Ewan to be able to spend time with his son and plan for the future.

With constant milk from a healthy local wet nurse, David soon began to put on weight. To the relief of all concerned, he also began to sleep well through the night.

Caroline having taken it upon herself to be his primary caregiver was thrilled at this unexpected development. She had fully expected to look like Hannah within a matter of days of taking over his care. Hannah, in turn, gave Caroline a look of thinly veiled disgust when she encountered her on the stairs one morning.

'Lady Caroline you are looking well, you look like you are well rested,' Hannah remarked.

Caroline beamed. 'Yes. David has taken well to my care. Last night he didn't even wake for his eleven o'clock feed.'

It was wonderful to feel needed. To have a purpose in someone's life. Caroline was fast gaining a taste for motherhood.

Her father and Ewan had offered to engage the services of a nursemaid, but Caroline wouldn't hear of it. David was family and therefore her responsibility. She would simply have to manage. Thousands of other women did, and so would she. She may have forgotten to mention to them that David was sleeping through the night and barely cried when he was with her.

If anyone was to have asked she would have claimed it as an unintended oversight on her part.

She delighted in spending time holding him in her arms and holding her nose close to his face as he slept. His newborn smell was intoxicating. She ran her fingertips over the dark tuft of hair which sat on his head.

'You are perfect my little man,' she whispered.

*　*　*

'Good morning,'

Ewan poked his head inside the nursery, a smile coming to his lips at the sight of Caroline holding David in her arms and cooing gently to him.

Caroline walked over to him and handed him his son.

'Support his head, by holding him this way,' she instructed.

The role of being a mother had it would appear come easily to Caroline.

He looked at her face. She was positively glowing with happiness. A look he had last seen on her face the night he took her to the opera. The last night they had spent together as a potential couple.

You threw a good woman away for the promise of unfettered sex. Admit it, Ewan Radley, you behaved as a blackguard.

'He looks as if he has put on weight,' he said.

'I think so. His wetnurse says she is struggling to keep up with his feeding demands. At this rate, I expect he will be on solid food before he is much older. Something tells me he will be a strapping lad and a fine figure of a man, just like his father,' she replied.

An awkward silence descended upon the room.

Ewan looked down at David, while Caroline fussed about with the peridot birthstone ring on her finger.

'My mother is pressing me to secure the services of a nursemaid for David. Not that you are not doing a sterling job, but she is firmly of the opinion that a young lady of your station should not be made to undertake the work of a maid. Considering I have no experience with regard to the raising of children, I have to listen and accept her counsel.

In the meantime, Hannah will take over some of the nursemaid duties. This will give you the opportunity to get out of this room for at least part of the day,' he said.

'Oh. I see,' she replied.

Disappointment echoed in her words, but Ewan pressed on.

'I would love to show you around the castle grounds and Strathmore Mountain. Besides, you and I haven't had an opportunity to talk since all this began. I think you would agree we have much to discuss.'

Caroline's face brightened at his offer, and Ewan took heart. If they could patch things up to the extent of actually being lukewarm friends again, he would consider himself most fortunate.

If he could manage at least that small miracle, who knew what else lay ahead for them. He would capitalize on every step forward.

'Scotland is at its very best when the early Winter colors are on display. The woods and the mountain are a wonderful palette of gold, brown and green at present. '

He pointed toward the window through which a thick wood was visible some half mile up the mountainside.

'Thank you, Ewan, I would like that very much,' she replied.

'It's wonderful up here. You can see for miles,' Caroline remarked.

She turned to see a red-faced Ewan struggling up the hill after her.

She stifled a satisfied grin at the sight of the duke huffing and puffing, while the climb had barely raised her heartbeat. Even in London, she walked long distances most days, rather than take the family carriage.

'I need to spend more time here. London has me bound to a desk and eating poorly,' said Ewan.

Caroline pulled an apple from the pocket of her skirts and broke it in half. She handed a piece to Ewan.

They walked on, quietly munching until they finally came to a stone bench deep in the woods. Caroline sat down and stretched out her legs. She patted the seat next to her.

'Sit. Rest. Catch your breath, Ewan.'

Here in this private place, she felt brave enough to use his first name. To show a familiarity she had once expected to be able to use with him by right of marriage.

Too much had now happened for her to care what he may think of her boldness.

'Thank you, Caroline.'

She pulled a piece of fruit cake, wrapped in cloth, from out of her other pocket and handed him a piece. The look of bemusement on his face brought forth a cheery laugh.

'No, I don't have half a side of lamb in my skirts. The cake is the last of the food I salvaged from breakfast. Cook gave me the cloth.'

'I'm sorry.'

She handed him the other piece of the cake, but he waved it away.

'I don't mean sorry about the food. I mean I am sorry for all that I have done to cause you pain and embarrassment. I treated you terribly and all you have done in return is be a rock of support. I don't deserve your good graces,' he said.

Caroline pushed her tongue against her lower teeth. She had rehearsed this scene in her mind so many times, that it felt like second nature. It was the oddest of feelings. At the very moment that the opportunity to tell him the depth of her heartache finally presented itself, she found herself backing away.

Railing against the past would serve no one.

'It is what it is. We cannot undo what has happened.'

Ewan reached out and took hold of Caroline's hand.

'I hope someday we can be friends,' he said.

Tears welled in her eyes as she pulled her hand away.

'I don't know. I am not certain that my charity can stretch that far. Ask me again in another few years, but only if you see me happily wed and with a husband who loves me. If I am not, then it would be best left in the past.'

She rose from the bench.

'I had better get back to the castle. David will be up from his sleep soon and if I am not there at feeding time to calm him down for the wet nurse, he will scream the house down.'

* * *

Ewan followed Caroline back to the castle keep.

He was about to apologize to her once more when she gave him a quick farewell wave and marched purposefully up the steps and into the Keep.

She hadn't actually accepted his first apology and he knew there was much she was holding back. As he watched her walk away, Ewan swore under his breath.

Only a fool would have thrown over a fine woman such as her for someone like Beatrice. And yet he had. While Caroline was a dark-haired English rose, her sister had been a flame haired temptress. Their short-lived affair had been full of passion, blazing rows, and soul changing sex.

After having taken her to his bed, he felt obliged to marry her. Beatrice was still the daughter of an earl. London society dictated that once he had known her in the biblical sense, she was his to marry and manage.

He hadn't managed her, nor got her to the altar. Instead, he had lost her and been handed his very own bastard child to raise. A scandalous mess.

'No Caroline. I'm not done. You will hear me out before you leave here. If I cannot have your friendship, I shall have your forgiveness,' he muttered after her.

He was determined to have that much before she left for home. Before she walked out of his life.

CHAPTER TWELVE

Ewan left the warm comfort of the downstairs sitting room early that evening.

Caroline had been mostly silent as they ate supper and had retired early claiming a headache. The presence of Aunt Maude and Lady Alison at the table restricted the conversation to that of social small talk and David's sleep patterns.

Once inside his bedroom, Ewan poured himself a glass of whisky from the fireside decanter and placed it on the bedside table. He kicked off his house shoes and lay back on the bed.

He was soon in a deep dream-filled slumber. His valet knocked several times before finally giving it up as a lost cause and heading to his own room.

In his dream, Ewan caught sight of a dark-haired woman in the distance. At first, he couldn't make her out, but as she slowly came into focus he knew her name.

'Caroline,' he murmured.

'Lord Strathmore,' she replied.

He snorted with frustration, much preferring her to call him by his Christian name.

She smiled. The dream Caroline could read his mind.

'Ewan. I know it pleases you when I call you Ewan. I expect there are other things I could do which would also please you,' she purred.

He pulled her roughly to him capturing her lips in a

searing kiss. She, in turn, slipped her hand down and unbuttoned the front placket of his trousers.

He groaned as she took a firm hold of him.

Dream sex was always wonderful. There were no rules, no strictures to delay the event. Women were willing and ready to do his bidding. He, in turn, was able to satisfy their every sexual need.

'I always knew you would be well endowed Ewan. I cannot wait until you are naked and on top of me. Let us not delay the pleasure any longer,' she whispered enticingly into his ear.

Asleep on the bed, Ewan rolled over and took hold of a large pillow. Holding it tightly against him, he continued to seduce the dream state, Caroline.

He tore open the top of her flimsy gown. It disappeared into thin air, leaving her naked form open to his gaze. Her perfectly formed breasts verily begged for his attention. Without hesitation, he bent down and took one of her peaked nipples into his mouth. When he sucked hard, she let out a deep sigh of pleasure.

She prised his fingers from her breast and went down on her knees before him, taking his swollen member into her mouth. When she sucked hard, Ewan thought he would go blind. She ran her tongue skillfully along the length of him, teasing him with her hot lips. He speared his hands through her hair as she ministered to his needs.

When he sensed he was on the verge of losing complete control, he slipped a thumb inside her mouth.

'Enough my beauty. It is your needs which should be attended to first.'

He pulled her to her feet and kissed her fiercely on the mouth. As he did so, his hands began to work their magic on her body. He slid a hand down her stomach and when he reached the folds of her intimate flesh, he slipped a thumb deep inside. She as wet as he was hard.

'Oh god Ewan, take me now. Ride me hard. You know I am ready for you.'

From out of the dream mist, a bed appeared and they were quickly upon it. He rose over her and kissed her once more. She guided him to her, arching back in the bed as he entered her willing body.

'Caroline. I have wanted you for so long. Lusted to take you as I am now.'

They were the last words he spoke before his sexually heated body took control of the dream. Thrusting repeatedly into the woman he loved, Ewan was lost in his desire to claim her. With her long legs wrapped around his upper thighs, he drove them both to the edge. Her sobs of pleasure and desperate need spurred him on to take her harder and deeper with every thrust. He wouldn't stop until he had sated her sexually until she had finally surrendered to him.

He thrust deep one last time and Caroline gave a guttural

cry as she came apart in his arms. His own roar of completion soon echoed in the bed.

* * *

Ewan woke early the next morning, still fully dressed. He rolled over onto his back and stared up at the ceiling.

Memories of his lust filled dream encounter with Caroline were foremost in his mind. He didn't need to touch himself to know he had woken with a serious case of morning glory.

The grandfather clock in the hall chimed the hour of seven. At seven thirty, his valet would be knocking on the door, expecting to enter and make preparations for Ewan's daily wardrobe.

He climbed off the bed and stripped off his clothes. His valet was a fastidious man and disapproved of his master sleeping fully clothed.

Now fully naked, and still hard as a rock Ewan slipped under the bedclothes. Taking himself in hand, he closed his eyes and slipped into the memory of his dream of Caroline.

CHAPTER THIRTEEN

While Ewan and Caroline quickly fell into the easy daily habit of taking a walk up the mountainside and into the woods. Ewan decided it wasn't prudent to further push the topic of their failed relationship any further at this time. Caroline for her part, he noted, seemed to have put the matter to the back of her mind.

She was holding David lovingly in her arms when Ewan arrived in the nursery several days later. She greeted him with a friendly smile.

'Good morning. Look, David, your papa has come to see you,' she said.

Ewan's heart swelled to see how natural the bond was between Caroline and his son. David began to fuss the instant she handed him to Hannah.

'Good morning to you too Lady Caroline. I was hoping we could take our daily walk again if you have time,' he replied.

She appeared to hesitate for a moment before replying.

'Yes of course. Give me a few minutes to get my things. I shall meet you outside near the kitchens.'

Ewan headed downstairs and waited for her. Standing outside in the fresh morning air, he pondered how he could once again broach the subject of their relationship. After the heated dream of the previous night, he knew he wanted more from her than her forgiveness.

It had only been after Beatrice had thrown him over that he had come to the awful realization that it was Caroline he had been in love with all along. The emotions he felt for her had been a long slow burn, not the all-consuming fire that had been his foolish notion of love with Beatrice.

He had allowed his lust to rule his actions and as a consequence had made the biggest mistake of his life. If he had kept to the path set for him, Caroline would be David's birth mother; and she would be his duchess.

Caroline appeared at the bottom of the stairs leading up from the kitchen, hurrying up them with more than her usual haste.

'Quick, before Cook catches us,' she laughed.

She flipped up the corner of her woolen cloak revealing a small wicker basket. She pushed the basket under Ewan's nose.

He caught sight of a freshly baked loaf of bread, a large piece of cheese and a knife. He nodded his approval. Caroline, it would appear had already captured the kitchen staff under her spell.

'Come on,' she said.

He followed her as she headed down across the courtyard and toward the small gate which led out into the fields beyond the castle. She had settled in quickly and was moving around the castle and grounds with the ease of someone who had long lived there.

'Beautiful day is it not?'

Ewan mumbled something in reply. His gaze was fixed firmly on the soft swing of Caroline's hips as she walked ahead of him. He longed to reach out and run his hand over her firm, round backside. What he would give to see the real-life Caroline do what her dream twin had done to him last night.

He swallowed deep.

There was only one way to find out.

Once inside the private space of the woods, they sat down and Caroline broke off a piece of the bread and handed it to Ewan. The aroma of fresh bread had his mouth watering.

He, in turn, took the knife and cut them both a generous chunk of the aged cheese.

'So good,' she murmured, between bites.

Ewan found his manhood go hard at the sound of her enjoyment. When she licked the crumbs from her fingers, he feared he may lose control.

'Caroline?'

'Mmm.'

He sat for a moment attempting to compose himself. The air between them had still not been cleared, and the dowager duchess had begun to make polite inquiries as to how long Ewan intended to keep Caroline at the castle.

He took a deep breath.

'It wasn't your fault that things did not go well between us, 'he said.

He cursed inwardly. That was not how he had planned to

start the conversation.

'What I meant was, that I am to blame for the situation that arose.'

'It's in the past, let us leave it there,' she replied.

She didn't look at him, rather her gaze appeared to be fixed firmly upon the branch of a nearby tree. The tension in her jaw the only outward sign of what he knew was her struggle to keep her emotions in check.

In a way Caroline was right. It would be easier to leave things in the past. But Ewan Radley was a stubborn man when it came to matters of the heart. The sure knowledge that he loved her had been growing steadily over the days since they had arrived at Strathmore Castle. If she felt anything for him, he was not going to let her keep it from him.

'I made a grave mistake in not allowing matters to fully develop between us. I am ashamed to say that I allowed your sister to turn my head.'

Caroline rose from the bench and turned to face him. She sucked in a deep breath before speaking.

'I think what you really mean to say, and correct me if I am wrong Ewan, was that you thought my sister capable of great passion. And since she and I were so unlike in nature, you, therefore, decided that I must be incapable of feeling and displaying such things,' she replied.

He shook his head.

'It's more complicated than that.'

She threw the remainder of her piece of bread and cheese into the nearby bushes.

'Actually, Ewan it's not. It's really quite simple. You chose her over me, the same as you chose lust over love. Have you ever considered why I find it hard to forgive the both of you? Beatrice was true to form, she saw something that could possibly be mine and set out to take it. You, in turn, decided that I could never hold your heart, that I was not worthy of your love. In your selfish pursuit of sexual pleasure, the pair of you dashed any hope I may have had for a happy marriage. You must pardon me if I struggle with more than a little bitterness over the injustice.'

She was right. He was the lowest cad alive. Having given Caroline every sign of his interest in her, he had won her heart, only to then without mercy crush it.

Violent shakes trembled through her body revealing to him the depth of the turmoil he had created in her life. Tears sprang to her eyes, but she wiped them hurriedly away.

Ewan rose to his feet and stretched out a hand. She stepped away.

'Don't. Don't you dare attempt to comfort me. I am not some weak female who you can cradle in your arms while she cries herself out, all because of loving you. Damn you, Ewan Radley. Is that the real reason why you brought me to Scotland? To see if you can try your hand with the other Hastings sister,' she ground out.

She went to step past him, but Ewan was quicker. He grabbed hold of Caroline's arm and swung her back to face him.

'I never wanted your tears.'

His fingers grasped hold of her hair; as he pulled her roughly to him. Hunger dictated his every move. Hunger for all that she could give.

'Let me go!'

'No.'

While it pained him to see her in such anguish, her tears signaled hope. If she no longer cared for him, she would not be so angry. He would kiss some sense into her if that is what it took.

His lips descended upon hers and he forced his tongue between her teeth. The challenge was laid down. Let her show him that she was immune to the heated passion which had been building up between them.

Caroline's initial stiffness in his arms soon faltered and she gave in to his desires. Her lips and tongue softened as their mouths engaged in a dance of ever-deepening passion. She groaned as he pulled her closer to him, hard against his body.

Innocent miss or not, he no longer cared to hide the physical effect she was having on him. It was time she understood what he had in mind for them.

His left hand drifted down and slipped under the flap of her cloak. Nimble fingers soon found the tight bud of her nipple. He gave it a gentle squeeze and was rewarded with yet another whimper of barely concealed delight. His dream was becoming reality.

He only had to hold her a little while longer in his sensual grip and she would be his to do with as he pleased. He could take her here and now, and she would let him. He would stake his claim to her body.

But not her heart, and for that, you will lose her forever.

The thought pulled him up sharp. He took his hand away and released her lips from his kiss.

Caroline stood staring at him, a look of pained confusion on her face.

'I shouldn't have done that,' he stammered.

He didn't get to finish the rest of what he meant to say, which was that he should have asked her permission first. Before he knew what had happened, Caroline had stepped forward and given him a resounding slap across the face.

'You are a heartless blackguard. You take what is not yours, and think that a feeble apology will smooth things over. You have no understanding of women Ewan. God have pity on the poor woman who is eventually saddled with the displeasure of being your wife!' she cried.

And with that, she was gone. Ignoring the established path by which they had come, Caroline crashed through the bushes and was quickly lost from sight.

'Oh,' was all that Ewan could manage, as his mind went into a whirl of indecision.

Should he follow her and try to make amends? Was he best to head back to the castle and see if he could intercept her as she returned? What if he did find her, what then would he say?

Caroline was right about one thing though, he didn't have a clue about women.

In anger and frustration, he turned and headed back down the path which led out of the woods. Instead of making amends and forging a new way forward with Caroline, all he had managed to do this day was push her further away and gain her enmity.

'Damn.'

Caroline reached the castle late that afternoon. She had spent the best part of four hours wandering the mountainside while trying to make sense of the morning's events.

Ewan had kissed her. He wanted her.

If she had stayed with him in the woods, matters between them would have likely taken the way of nature. She had for a moment been tempted to let him have his way. To allow them both the pleasures her heated body craved. Yielding to his demands would have been the easiest of choices.

Caroline Hastings, was, however, a woman capable of seeing the repercussions of taking the easy path in life. She was not about to make that mistake.

Knowing Ewan and both their social stations, he would have offered marriage as soon as he caught sight of her naked breast. And he would be exactly where he had been with her sister. Compelled to marry a girl whom he didn't love. It would be the rocky start to a marriage doomed to failure.

She stifled a satisfied snort at the thought of having slapped his face. As a duke, it was not likely something which happened to Ewan Radley on a regular basis. The shock on his face had been real enough.

'Caroline?'

She turned to see Lady Alison standing in the doorway of her sitting room.

'A letter has arrived for you from your father.'

* * *

Back in her own room, Caroline opened the letter, read its brief contents and then without further thought screwed it up into a ball and threw it into the fireplace.

As expected Lord Hastings had made his position clear. Caroline had overstayed her time in Scotland, she was now commanded to return home to Hastings Hall as soon as possible.

As she watched the flames burn up the letter, Caroline felt a sense of calm come over her.

Her father was right. She had no right to linger any longer in Scotland. Other than as a sometime relative in David's life she was a stranger in this landscape.

In Ewan's world, she was just another problem, something which he felt he needed to rectify. Kissing her had simply been his clumsy way of attempting to smooth things over between them.

'He doesn't love me. The only reason he asked me to come to Scotland was to ensure he enjoyed a quiet journey home and to get David away from prying eyes as soon as possible.'

She could consider her task complete. She had seen her nephew home to Scotland and into the capable arms of his grandmother and paternal great aunt.

It was time for her to go home, mourn Beatrice in whatever way she could and get on with her life.

'When did Caroline say that she intended to depart for ent?'

Lady Alison finished spreading the marmalade onto her orning bread before setting down the knife.

'A week, perhaps two. But she did say it had to be by the econd week of December at the latest. She wants to be home in ime for Christmas,' Lady Alison replied.

She and Aunt Maude were enjoying an indulgent late reakfast, some three days after Caroline had received the issive from her father. Caroline herself had gone for her now sual solo morning ramble, up the mountain.

'That boy of yours is a bloody fool,' Aunt Maude replied.

The dowager duchess sat quiet, patiently waiting for the est of Aunt Maude's speech.

'He brought her all the way up here for a reason, and hat reason certainly wasn't to show her the sights of trathmore Mountain. If she had wanted rocks and mountains she ould have gone to the Peak District.'

'And what do you suggest I do about it Maude dearest? I ave tried to reason with him. I was the one, if you recall, ho told him to stay away from the eldest of the Hastings irls in the first place. Beatrice was trouble from the day he was born, anyone with a seeing eye could tell that,' Lady lison replied.

Speaking ill of the dead did not sit well with her, but there was no point in dancing around the fact that Beatrice Hastings had been an unruly child who had grown to be a headstrong, untamed young woman.

The only thing of value Beatrice had managed to achieve in her short life, was to give birth to a son. A child, Lady Alison, was now tasked with helping to raise.

'We could work to ensure that she doesn't leave,' replied Maude.

It had been several centuries since the castle had last held prisoners.

'The windlass still works. I could have the drawbridge raised. Then again from the look on your face, I am assuming you already have something planned.'

Lady Alison looked up and found herself staring at Aunt Maude who was leaning forward in her chair, a look of expectation on her face.

'What do you mean?' she replied.

Aunt Maude harrumphed in disgust.

'You have a sly grin on your face, and you only ever have one of those when you are plotting something,' replied Maude.

Lady Alison chortled.

'I am sure that if you and I put our heads together, we could find a dozen different ways to ensure that Lady Caroline remains at Strathmore Castle.'

CHAPTER SIXTEEN

Until Beatrice Hastings came hurtling into his life Ewan Radley had held fast onto the opinion that he was not a foolish man. After she left him with his self-respect in tatters mere months later, he was forced to accept that perhaps he was not as worldly nor clever as he had once thought.

The same feeling began to seep once more into his mind. His encounter with Caroline had been a disaster. One minute he was exulting in having her submit to his sensual overtures, the next he was in shock having received a slap to his face delivered with great fury.

He sat and stared at the glass of whisky in his hand. He had already downed two large glasses of Scotland's finest single malt and was steadily working his way through a third. The buzz in the back of his brain had become an uncomfortable mixture of alcohol and regret.

Caroline didn't want him in her life. She wasn't prepared to forgive him. Perhaps it was time to move on and find a woman who would make a sensible wife. A woman who would take on both the role of Duchess of Strathmore and stepmother without fuss. He could settle for the traditional *ton* marriage. He would be a comfortable husband with a comfortable wife.

He sat the glass down. The fight was not yet over. Getting drunk wouldn't solve any of his problems.

CHAPTER SEVENTEEN

With only a matter of days until she was intending to depart, Caroline decided she must take her leave on better terms with the Radley family.

It was after she had spent the best part of three days avoiding Ewan that Caroline decided she was being immature about the situation.

Discounting how uneasy the situation with Ewan currently was, there was a real danger that if she wasn't able to come to an amicable accord with David's family, she may never see her nephew again. If she had to swallow her hurt and pride, to ensure she remained part of his life, then that was what she would do.

'Do you have a moment?'

Lady Alison and Aunt Maude, whom Caroline suspected were joined at the hip, were seated reading in the castle's library.

'Yes, of course, my dear, come in, take a seat,' Lady Alison replied.

Caroline sat down on a long dark brown leather couch and rested her hands in her lap. During the night she had come up ith a plan, which hopefully would go some way to repairing

atters.

'I have been led to believe that you don't celebrate

hristmas as such in Scotland.'

'Yes. Well, the church here has had some issues with it.

hen we are at the castle for Christmas, we reserve our major

elebrations of the season for Hogmanay at New Years. Pity you

ouldn't stay long enough to see it. Why do you ask?'

'I would like. If you are agreeable. To visit the village

nd arrange to purchase Christmas gifts for you all. While I

yself, will not be here on the day in question, it would make

e happy to know that you at least have a small reminder of me

t that time. I, in turn, shall drink a toast to your good

ealth at my family's Christmas Dinner in Kent,' replied

aroline.

Aunt Maude put down her book. She was out of her chair

nd had her hands on Caroline's shoulders before Lady Alison

ad the opportunity to reply.

'A capital idea, Caroline. I shall go and get my cloak,'

he said.

***

Less than an hour later, Aunt Maude led a warmly dressed,

ut slightly bemused Caroline out of the castle and across the

uge wooden drawbridge. Trips to the various shops in London

ere usually planned days ahead of time, but having found

erself caught up in Maude's *carpe diem* attitude to shopping,

Caroline decided to go along.

They headed down the road which led to the nearby village of Strathmore.

There had been a heavy snowfall during the night. Snow was piled up on the embankments on either side of the road.

As the warmth of the morning sun slowly melted the snow, sections of the road turned into large water-filled potholes.

'Mind how you go lass, this road can be a wee bit treacherous after a snowfall,' cautioned Maude.

Caroline deftly sidestepped one hole but failed to miss a second. After several of these mishaps, her walking boots were both soaked through.

'I don't suppose you are used to these sorts of roads in England. It pays not to wear your good clothes when you are out and about hereabouts. I myself save my nice slippers for the season in London, and my good old Tackety boots for winter here.'

Maude lifted her skirts to reveal a pair of mud-covered, black hobnail boots. She was the epitome of practicality.

'We should get you a pair.'

Caroline laughed. She liked Aunt Maude immensely. A good plain-speaking Scottish woman with a heart of gold. Maude's sudden insistence on being the one to accompany Caroline to the village was an unexpected, but welcome surprise.

They reached the end of the road and entered the main street of the village of Strathmore. Aunt Maude stopped

utside a long stone building with a bright green shingle
anging outside.

'Welcome to Dunn's. If you cannot get what you need here,
'm afraid you will have to go to Edinburgh.'

Caroline followed her inside.

Within a short time, she had found most of what she
eeded. Fine lambswool with which to knit new scarves for the
adies. Some heavy cotton fabric to make clothes for David,
ho was rapidly outgrowing the clothes she had purchased for
im in Manchester. That only left Ewan.

She wandered around the store for some time, picking up
nd putting down various items.

She was close to buying Ewan a collection of poems by
obert Burns, which she suspected he already owned when Aunt
aude came to her rescue.

'If you are looking for something for himself, then you
ould always make him a shirt,' she said.

Caroline considered the suggestion for a second. A shirt
ade perfect sense. It was practical, and being skilled with a
eedle and fine thread she knew she could manage to make a
uality garment within a matter of days. In the time left, she
ould embroider some fancy work on the cuffs.

'Thank you, Maude, that is just what I need.'

After paying for her purchases and having them wrapped
he and Maude made their way out of the shop. As they left,
aroline missed seeing the secret smile that passed between

Aunt Maude and the proprietor, Mr. Dunn.

CHAPTER EIGHTEEN

As soon as they returned to the castle, Caroline set about making her Christmas gifts. With good humor and best wishes in every stitch, she soon had completed two long elegant scarves. One each for Lady Alison and Aunt Maude.

Two days later she began to cut the linen for Ewan's shirt, but oddly found herself in tears every time she set the shears to the fabric. Eventually, she put the shirt to one side and set about making David's gift.

She was busily marking out the pattern for a smock for David, skillfully using tailor's chalk, when there was a knock at her bedroom door.

'Just a moment,' she called out.

Picking up the smock, she quickly stuffed it into a drawer. While she wouldn't be present when the gifts were opened, she still wanted to know that they would be a surprise or all their recipients.

The door opened, and Ewan stepped across the threshold.

'Oh, hello,' she said.

They stood in awkward silence for a moment, before he
inally spoke.

'I came to apologize.'

She shrugged her shoulders. He had already tried to
pologize, and things had not turned out well.

'I know things will never be right between us again, and
accept full responsibility for that unfortunate situation.
ut.'

'What?'

He puffed out his cheeks.

'I need your help. I promise I wouldn't be here if there
as any other way. And, since it does directly involve David,
thought you might see your way to put the other matters to
ne side and assisting me.'

The look of desperation on Ewan's face reminded her of
hen he begged her to come to Scotland. A man floundering in a
redicament. He clearly didn't want to ask for her help; he
ad explored all other options before coming to seek her
ssistance.

'I'm listening,' she replied.

The fact that she had not said a flat out no, seemed to
park his mood. He gave a small sigh of relief.

'My mother has arranged for a group of young ladies from

Edinburgh to visit the castle tomorrow. Hopefully, from that cohort, a suitable nursemaid for David will be selected. For some reason known only to herself, my mother has recused herself from the interview process. How she could possibly have chosen the candidates and then claimed a possible conflict of interest, I do not understand. And before you ask, Aunt Maude has suddenly come down with some form of mystery illness and is also unable to assist with the interviews,' he said.

Caroline pursed her lips. The fact that she was even further down the list of suitable helpers than unwed Aunt Maude was an unexpected blow to her pride. It was she, not Aunt Maude, who had nursed David for most of the days since they rescued him from the boarding house in Manchester.

You did decide to put your own interests aside and do what is best for the boy. Why else would you have agreed to come to Scotland?

Her wounded pride would have to heal itself. There was a job to be done.

'Yes, of course, I will help.'

* * *

'You do realize that between the two of us, we have little to no experience in hiring a nursemaid, let alone raising a child. I still cannot fathom why Lady Alison didn't wish to partake of the interviews, she at least has had the xperience of being a real mother,' said Caroline.

Ewan sat his cup of coffee down. While he couldn't
nderstand his mother's reasoning, it at least afforded him
he opportunity to spend some precious time with Caroline.
ime, he knew was fast running out.

'Well we shall just have to make the best of things and
opefully one of the girls will be suitable. With eight to
hoose from, the odds should be favorable,' he replied.

In the end, he was more than relieved that it was
aroline who he managed to press into service for the
nterviews. He quickly discovered that she and he were much
like as to the qualities they were seeking in a nursemaid for
avid.

All afternoon they sat side by side interviewing the
rospective nursemaids. As the last of the eight candidates
alked out of the room, they looked at one another and shook
heir heads.

'I know Mama did her best to source the girls, but not
ne of them appealed to me. I wouldn't want any of them
aising my son. What do you think?' he said.

The day had been long and at times confronting. Two of
he prospective candidates had taken their leave when they
iscovered that they would be nursemaid to an illegitimate
hild. One had even suggested that she could catch something
nholy from a bastard.

It had taken all of Ewan's self-control not to strike the

woman when she told him his son was the product of the devil's sin in the world.

Caroline shifted in her seat and looked at him.

'I must confess I am in complete agreement with you. You may need to go to Edinburgh yourself and source the right woman. Time is becoming of the essence. If Hannah and I are to make it back to Hastings Hall for Christmas, we shall need to leave within the next few days,' she replied.

The afternoon had been a complete waste of time with regard to sourcing a nursemaid, but at least matters between Caroline and himself had settled down enough for them to be able to speak honestly with one another. Not settled enough though, that he felt that he could once more tread the dangerous ground of telling her he loved her.

The poor showing of the candidates only delayed her departure. At some point, a suitable nursemaid would be found, and he would be left facing the inevitable goodbye. Caroline had made her position regarding their relationship all too clear.

As Caroline went back to her room, Ewan headed out into the castle courtyard. He needed some fresh air to clear his mind and humor.

The eight unsuccessful nursemaid candidates were milling around in a circle awaiting the Strathmore travel coach which would take them back to Edinburgh.

As he drew closer, Ewan noticed an odd thing. Each of the

irls was holding a small coin purse in their hands. All
ight-coin purses were identical in color and size. Catching
ight of him, they quickly put their hands in their skirt
ockets. Not one of them dared to meet his gaze.

Realization slipped quietly into his mind.

Ewan smelt a rat.

CHAPTER NINETEEN

The rat, or rather a pair of rats in question, he sensed,
ould be found in his mother's sitting room. He marched
ngrily back into the castle keep.

Upon entering his mother's sitting the room, he saw that
he previously indisposed Aunt Maude was happily tucking into
large piece of cake and a slice of cheese. Seated beside her
n the couch was his mother, enjoying an early afternoon

brandy.

They were celebrating.

He closed the door behind him, and strode into the middle of the room. With hands on hips, he stopped and faced them.

'Ewan my dear boy, how did the interviews go?' asked Lady Alison, nonchalantly.

He would have laughed at her pathetic attempt at disinterest if he hadn't been so furious. By meddling in matters, his mother and Maude were only making the situation with Caroline more precarious.

'Yes, did you choose one?' added Maude, before stuffing a piece of cake into her mouth. She sat back on the couch and smiled at him.

Ewan had to give Maude her dues. She at least attempting to call his bluff. He of course wasn't having any of it.

Between the two of them, the Radley women had somehow managed to bribe the potential nursemaids, and ensure that every last one of them had thrown the interview.

'I am not here to play games ladies. I know what the pair of you have done. I saw the coin purses. Did you really think I wouldn't unearth your scheme? The smart plan would have been to wait until they got back to Edinburgh before you paid them off.'

The women exchanged an uneasy look. Lady Alison took a leisurely sip of her brandy before setting the glass down with slow purpose.

'We were only trying to help. You don't seem to be making much headway in getting Caroline's agreement to stay, so we decided you needed a little nudge,' she replied.

Ewan sighed. He understood that they had good intentions. That they did not seem to appreciate, was that Caroline wasn't a woman to be manipulated. If she had any inkling as to what Lady Alison and Aunt Maude were up to, she would be on the first coach out of Strathmore Castle and he would never see her again.

He had barely made headway with her since the incident in the woods, and the thought that his mother and aunt were trying to play cupid had his blood running cold with fear.

'I must insist that you cease and desist from trying to help forthwith. This situation is a far more complicated and delicate one than either of you seem to comprehend,' he replied.

The two women looked down at the floor, crestfallen.

'We are truly sorry,' they replied in unison.

Ewan felt like an utter heel at making his mother and Maude apologize. Their intentions had been for the good. He made a mental note to make it up to them as soon as he could.

His greatest concern at this point was ensuring that Caroline didn't discover the truth of the afternoon she had wasted.

'Thank you, ladies. I shall leave you to your brandy and vittles.'

He turned on his heel and marched from the room, intent on making sure that the travel coach to Edinburgh left without further delay.

As soon as he was gone, Lady Alison turned to Aunt Maude.

'Well, Ewan couldn't have been plainer in his words. We are to stay out of matters that do not concern us.'

Aunt Maude brushed the cake crumbs from her fingers and picked up her glass of brandy. After slurping down a large gulp, she held it in her hands.

'So, what do you suggest we do now?' she replied.

A sly smile danced its way across Lady Alison's lips.

'The matter of my grandson and any future grandchildren of the Radley line directly concerns me. As such, I feel it well within my rights to meddle. We are going to move onto the next part of our plan. Caroline has one obvious weak spot and we need to fully exploit it. It's time to roll our secret weapon out onto the battlefield.'

The sound of the two brandy glasses being clinked together sounded in the room.

'Let us drink a toast to David Radley and the hope that he can save us all.'

CHAPTER TWENTY

Ewan lay in his bed in the early hours of the morning, listening to the storm which had sprung up earlier during the previous day and had continued unabated. Gale force winds ashed heavy rain against the window. It was not unheard of

or these storms to continue for days on end at this time of

he year. Heavy snow would soon follow. Roads would become

mpassible and no one would be traveling from the castle

As he rolled over and attempted to go back to sleep, he

uttered a single prayer.

Lord let it rain for forty days and forty nights.

***

The rain eventually subsided later that morning, sparing

hem all from a great flood. The roads around the village and

astle, however, did not escape unscathed. The bridge on the

ain road leading back to Falkirk was partly washed away. When

is steward returned to the castle later that afternoon, he

as the bearer of bad news.

'It will be days before anyone can get near to pulling

he pylons back into place, your Grace. The ground around the

ottom of the bridge is a quagmire at best,' his steward

nnounced.

'Yes, and the clouds have changed from being rain clouds

o low snow bearing ones. We may have a long wait before we

an get those repairs done,' Ewan replied.

He would not risk the lives of his workers trying to fix

he bridge. The village and castle had plenty of provisions

nd winter stores of food. If they had to last well into the

ew year being cut off from the rest of the world, it wouldn't

e the first time.

After his steward took his leave, Ewan stood and looked
out the window. He looked up at the clouds which sat over the
top of Strathmore Mountain. They were so low, that the top of
the mountain had completed disappeared.

He bowed his head.

'Thank you, Lord, I will not waste this blessing.'

* * *

'How long did you say?'

Ewan did his best to keep calm.

Caroline's reaction to being told that the bridge near
Torwood was gone; and that she may be staying at the castle
indefinitely, was not unexpected.

'Is there no other road I could take?'

'I'm afraid not, the only other road leads toward the
Highlands and that is already covered in several feet of snow.
It will be impassable until the Spring. You must grant that we
are a long way from the cobbled streets of Edinburgh or
London,' Ewan replied.

He wracked his brains, looking for anything he could say
to placate her.

'At least you will be here for David's christening,' he
said.

His mother had raised the question of David's baptism
late the previous evening. He hadn't given the idea much
thought at the time, thinking it the least of his concerns,
but now suddenly it was right in front of him. The thought

ent straight to his lips.

He was only beginning to absorb the words he had just
poken when Caroline's face lit up with joy.

'Oh Ewan, that would be lovely. I hadn't thought about
is baptism, but now that you mention it, I think it's
onderful. What a timely idea,' she replied.

He smiled. Both at the obvious pleasure the invitation
ad given to Caroline, and to the fact that his mother had
layed a sly hand and got him to do her bidding.

Touché, Mama.

CHAPTER TWENTY-ONE

Caroline and the two Radley women were seated at breakfast the next morning when Ewan arrived in the breakfast room. He came to Lady Alison and brushed a kiss on her cheek.

'All arranged then?' she asked.

'Yes. Christmas Eve. Now just to secure the services of another godparent and everything will be ready.

He looked over at Caroline and smiled.

'I have already asked Aunt Maude to be one of David's godparents, I would like very much for you to also be a godparent.'

His offer took her by surprise. She hadn't really thought about who David's godparents would be. For that matter, she wasn't entirely sure of the church's position regarding illegitimate children. The fact that David was to be baptized within the grounds of his family seat, likely negated any issues that may have existed with the Church of Scotland.

'Are you certain?'

'Why not? You would make a perfect godmother for David. And it would mean that his mother's side would be represented somewhat in a formal position in his life,' he replied.

'What an unexpected honor. I accept of course. Who is to be his godfather?'

'I would have asked my brother, but he is in London and wouldn't be able to make the ceremony. The church doesn't llow godparents by proxy. The village minister said that as I

m his father I am well within my rights to be his godfather.

t means that my name and his will at least be together in the

amily and church records somewhere. I owe my firstborn son

hat much.'

Caroline felt tears well up inside of her. Ewan was doing

is utmost to be a good father, and to respect Beatrice's

emory. It too would be nice to know that her own name would

e alongside both Ewan and David Radley's names in the church

ecords.

Being present for David's baptism was a nice consolation

or not making it home to Kent for Christmas. The heavy

nowfalls and damaged bridge at Torwood were perhaps a

lessing after all.

***

Christmas Eve dawned with gray skies. Low clouds hung

ver the valley. Strathmore Mountain was completely hidden

rom view. The air in the castle courtyard was bitingly cold.

tanding on the steps of the keep, rugged up against the

hill, Caroline wrapped her cloak about her. There were small

ockets of snow all around the yard.

Aunt Maude joined her, and looked up at the sky.

'Beautiful Scottish morning my dear. Perfect weather,'

he remarked.

Caroline glanced at her, unsure if Ewan's aunt was being

bsurd or truly meant it. The Scots seemed to find joy in the very worst of weather.

'We've had more snow by the look of it,' Caroline
replied.

'Aye, we had a good three inches of it last night. Cook
tells me that the road up from the village is deadly with
black ice. But rest assured that won't stop the minister. As
they say, it's not the weather that is wrong, but the clothes
you are wearing.'

Lady Alison and Ewan appeared behind them in the doorway.
Ewan was dressed in the Strathmore tartan of black, gray and
blue. A silver kilt pin, with the family crest of a rearing
horse, mounted over three, four-pointed stars, sat on the
lower corner of his kilt. It shone as brightly as the dull
morning light would permit. With a basket-hilted sword hanging
by his side, he looked every inch the true Scottish Laird.

In his arms, wrapped warmly in a thick tartan blanket,
was David. He was awake; and to Caroline's observant eye, was
taking it all in.

'Come on then my lad, let's get you churched,' said Ewan.

With that Ewan and the small christening party set off
across the courtyard and toward the small stone chapel which
sat within the castle grounds. As they walked, the collective
staff of the castle stood to one side. Hats off and heads
bowed.

Caroline watched them as she walked by. She was filled
with an overwhelming sense of relief. The people of Strathmore

astle had accepted David as one of them. He would never be

heir lord, but to them, he was still a son of the house.

The christening party gathered inside the small stone

hapel.

It was a simple building, with an ornamental archway just

nside the door. Aunt Maude explained that it dated from a

ime when Scotland was still officially a Roman Catholic

ountry. Down the generations, and changes of national faith,

he family had never seen any particular need to make

lterations to the building. It was still a house of God, so

hey had left it as it was originally built.

The minister from the village was waiting inside.

'Welcome your Graces, Lady Maude, Lady Hastings, would

ou please gather round'.

There was a small area to one side of the altar, in which

he baptismal font was located. The small party managed to

queeze inside the area without too much discomfort.

Beginning with Ewan, they all took turns to hold David

nd make their vows to be good godparents and support David in

is life. When it came time for Caroline to make her vows,

wan handed the now sleeping David to her.

Tears immediately sprang to her eyes. She was about to

ow to help raise him, yet there was every chance she wouldn't

lay much of a role in his life. She turned to Ewan.

'Ewan, as you have chosen me to be David's godmother,

hat means I must be a part of his life as he grows up.

Promise you will allow me to fulfill my vows. Don't shut me out his life, or yours for that matter. Your future duchess will have to understand that I have a role to play in my nephew's life,' she said.

He stepped forward and placed a fatherly kiss on his son's forehead.

'I promise never to take your Aunt Caroline from you, my lad,' he said.

Lady Alison reached out and patted Caroline's arm. 'We all promise.'

As soon as the sun had begun to set, a large bonfire in
he center of the courtyard was lit. Villagers and castle
taff alike crowded around the giant fire and watched as the
irst sparks drifted up into the night air.

To one side of the bonfire, a giant spit had been
onstructed. Two huge boars had been roasting on the spit
ince just after sunrise. The heady smell of roast meat
ermeated the air.

No one would be going to bed hungry this night.

Ewan stood on the steps of the keep and watched as a
arge wagon was hauled into place well away from the fire.
mall children were gathered up by their parents and taken to
 safe distance. At his signal, the first of many fireworks
ere lit and roared into the night sky.

Loud cheers and applause greeted every new rocket as it
eaded skyward. Squeals of delight soon followed as the
ockets exploded high overhead.

Ewan silently congratulated himself for having managed to
rrange David's christening on Christmas Eve. The fireworks
nd festivities served both purposes well.

'Where is Caroline?' asked Lady Alison.

He turned around, and for the first time since arriving
or the festivities realized that Caroline was not present at
he gathering.

'I don't know, I haven't seen her since we came back from David's christening. She did promise to join us this evening,' he replied.

Caroline had been glowing with pride, and he suspected happiness when they returned to the keep following the christening. It had been a stroke of genius for Lady Alison and Aunt Maude to suggest having Caroline as David's godmother. She was now forever linked as family to her nephew.

He searched over the heads of the milling household staff gathered on the steps behind him, but could not see Caroline's tall, slender form. He had just decided to go in search of her when she suddenly appeared to one side of the doorway.

He beckoned for her to join him, but she shook her head.

Something was wrong.

'Mama, would you please take over from me, I need to speak to Caroline.'

As soon as he reached her side, he could see Caroline was troubled. Even in the fading light, he could discern the telltale puffy eyes of one who had not long ago finished weeping.

Whatever was the matter, the middle of a crowd was not the place to press her for an answer.

'Come with me,' he said, taking her gently by the arm.

Ewan led her through the keep and up a long set of winding stairs, finally reaching a small doorway, which he pushed open. Beyond the door was the ramparts at the top of he castle. A private place that only the Radley family embers were ever permitted to visit.

He closed the door behind them.

'We are alone, and no one will dare disturb us,' he said.

Caroline wiped tears away from her face, refusing Ewan's utstretched hand of comfort.

'I am fine. I think I am almost done with crying for this vening thank you,' she replied.

A chill breeze rippled along the top of the battlements nd she wrapped her cloak more tightly about herself. Ewan eached into his coat pocket and drew out a whisky flask. He ffered it to her.

'Glenturret whisky, a fine drop. Get a dram or two of hat into you to ward off the night air. Then we can talk.'

She took the flask from his hand and took a sip.

'That is good. A bit smoother than brandy. Thank you.'

She handed the flask back to Ewan, after which she pulled letter from out of her skirt pocket.

'Hannah gave this to me when we were in Manchester. It's rom Beatrice. To tell the truth, I had forgotten about it, ut I was rummaging through my things this afternoon, looking or something to wear for Christmas Day when I came across it. regretted opening it from the moment I started reading.'

Ewan wracked his brains. What on earth could Beatrice ave possibly said to Caroline to make her so upset? What was he final piece of the Beatrice puzzle which had been laid in place to bring them all down?

He held the letter up against one of the arrow loops of the battlements, accessing the light given off by the giant bonfire below. When he was finally finished reading, he slowly folded the letter and stuffed it into his coat pocket. Sickened in his heart, he never intended that Caroline would ever have possession of it again.

'I am so terribly sorry Caroline. I had no idea.'

The letter was full of fury and vitriol. Hatred for both Ewan and their unborn child was laid bare on the page. But, Beatrice had saved the blackest of her hatred for her sister. Caroline had borne the full brunt of it.

'I knew she always resented me. As a child growing up I sensed she wished I was not in her life. By the time we became adults, we barely had any sort of relationship, but even I never suspected the true depth of her enmity toward me. That she would deliberately poison any chance that you and I had of being together.'

A cold sensation landed heavily in Ewan's stomach.

Beatrice hadn't set out to seduce him, rather she had determined to destroy her sister by whatever means necessary. He had merely been a pawn in her wicked game. A blind and selfish pawn.

Worst of all, the very child which had grown within her womb meant less than nothing to her. David's very existence was a bane in her life.

'I don't know what to say. There is nothing that I can ever do to make amends for the hurt I have caused,' he stammered.

He watched with interest as an unexpected smile came to her lips. Her whole face changed as the sadness lifted.

'I thought that myself. For the longest time this afternoon, I was lost in the depth of despair. I wept for all the long years of my sister being my enemy. Of the sisterly affection so willingly withheld. Painful regrets that threatened to cut me to the core.

But no more. For you see, in the recent hours I came to an understanding of what she did. I've read that letter a dozen times; and by searching my soul, I discovered the truth. By seducing you and thereby tearing us asunder, she thought the damage would be permanent. That the fabric of you and I could never be repaired. But she didn't count on one thing; the power of forgiveness.'

Caroline came to Ewan's side and tenderly placed her hand on his cheek.

'If I was never to forgive you, she would have won. Her victory against me complete. Today we both made vows to David and to each other, and that has opened my heart once more to you. I forgive you, Ewan.'

CHAPTER TWENTY-THREE

Caroline hadn't meant to reveal all to Ewan this night, she had planned to make it a slow unveiling of her heart, but seeing him in the pale light she realized the time was ripe.

'Caroline,' he murmured.

A strong hand came around her waist and pulled her toward him. For a moment they searched one another's gazes. The time was beyond words. So much had already been said.

She lifted her lips to his as he took her mouth in a scorching kiss. His previous attempts to kiss her had been polite, almost apologetic. This kiss was an act of affirmation. She was his. She exulted in the certainty that Ewan was holding nothing back.

He deepened the kiss as his tongue swept into her mouth. Caroline groaned and returned the passion in kind. She was an innocent in the world of love, but she was a fast learner.

As she yielded to his demands, she claimed victory. He

as hers from this moment on. She slipped her hands inside
wan's coat and wrapped her arms around his waist. She had
aited such a long time for this moment, she never intended to
et go.

They broke the kiss for the briefest of moments as the
oud bang of a large firework exploding overhead shook the
ight. Within a second, their lips were reunited in a second
iss, as hot and fierce as the first.

She relaxed into the kiss, savoring every moment.

After all that had come between them, Caroline wasn't the
east surprised when she felt hot tears run down her cheeks.

Ewan pulled away, his gaze desperately searching hers,
eeking answers.

'Why are you crying?'

She shook her head. Her tears were no longer through
nguish, but rather from the utter relief that this moment had
ctually happened. So many nights over the past year she had
ain awake and pondered events. Over and over in her mind, she
ad wondered where she had gone wrong. At what point had Ewan
ealized he did not love her. How if she had played the game
ith more skill, could she have secured his love for her very
wn. Questions which at times had threatened her sanity.

'I just never thought we would ever get a second chance.
didn't think you wanted me.'

Someday, many years from now, she would reveal to him how
eep was her despair the night Beatrice came home and

announced that she seduced the very man Caroline loved. For now, she would let it lay in the past, tonight she was happy to let the tears fall.

As long as Ewan continued to kiss her, Caroline didn't care.

★★★

Ewan escorted Caroline back to the festivities. Neither dare look at the other for fear of revealing their recent occupation.

A fiddler appeared and began to play. The castle servants gathered round and in pairs danced a lively jig.

Hannah holding baby David in her arms, laughed with delight.

'Look, David, look at all those people dancing. I bet when you grow up to be a man, you will be a fine dancer. You will go to all the finest parties and balls in London,' she said.

Ewan looked across at Caroline. She was smiling and tapping her toes. He could see she was itching to get out and dance a jig with the others. Polite society dictated that as their lord, he shouldn't mingle with the staff. It went against all propriety for them to see him as one of them.

A sharp elbow in the ribs from Aunt Maude gave him the reminder that he was lord of the castle and he could do as he pleased.

'Get out there my lad, and take your wee lassie with ya.'

Ewan took hold of Caroline's hand and pulled her into the crowd. The gathered onlookers clapped and cheered with unrestrained delight.

'I can't remember the last time I danced a country jig,' Caroline said with a laugh.

Ewan swung her around and lifted her into the air. His hands fitting around her waist as if they had been designed for one another. As he set her back down, he saw the pure joy in her face.

If they hadn't been in the middle of the courtyard with a hundred pair of eyes all turned in their direction, he would have kissed her again there and then.

'You had better get used to it, these folks love any excuse for a jig,' he said.

CHAPTER TWENTY-FOUR

As the bonfire died down, the crowd dispersed and the villagers made their way home.

Snow flurries now danced about the courtyard in their own elegant fashion. Another night of snow beckoned.

Inside the castle, Ewan made his way to the strong room. A heavy iron door protected the front of the family vault. It took two hands and a goodly portion of his strength to pull the door open.

Inside the strong room was a series of shelves. There were various sealed envelopes and roles of parchment on the high shelves. Included in them were the original letters patent for the first Duke of Strathmore.

He stood for a moment. In this private place, he could acknowledge the great gift and burden which had been passed down through the generations to him. Strathmore was his to hold. His life's task was to increase its wealth and power for future generations.

With his private reflection over, Ewan went in search of his quarry. On the middle shelf sat a set of red velvet boxes. Each one containing a priceless piece of family jewelry. He picked up a small red ring box and opened it.

Inside, held neatly in the ring holder was a gold ring. A bright ruby, surrounded by diamonds was set in a simple, but elegant design.

The ring was nearly two hundred years old. James the first, King of the combined crowns of England and Scotland had lifted it to the Radley family as payment for their support of him during the early years of his reign.

He took the ring from the box and held it up to the light. The fire within it burned bright, offset by the clear glow of the diamonds. It was worth a princely fortune in any man's mind.

Tonight, Caroline had made her position clear. Now it was time for him to take control and move matters forward. The greatest risk as he saw it at this point, was to offer up the ring, and for Caroline to reject it.

Caroline Hastings was not the sort of girl to have her head turned by a jewel, no matter how magnificent it was. The Hastings were not short on heirlooms of their own.

He knew she wanted more from him than mere titles and jewels. She sought the most precious treasure he held.

His heart.

He put the ring back in the box and snapped the lid shut.

The situation was absurd. There were a hundred women of good families he could call on this very night and have them accept his proposal of marriage. Dukes were not inclined to beg women to marry them.

But the more he thought about it, the more certain he was that if it came to it, he would beg Caroline to be his wife.

It was time to tell her he loved her.

CHAPTER TWENTY-FIVE

Caroline wrapped her long black travel cloak around her and pulled the hood over her head.

What she would actually say to anyone she encountered in the keep if she was discovered, she hadn't decided.

With the snow now falling at a steady rate, few would believe that she was intent on taking a late night's walk in the castle grounds.

Reaching Ewan's bedroom door, she knocked.

'I won't be needing anything further this evening,' he said, opening the door.

He was clad only in a shirt.

The look of surprise on his face at his visitor being Caroline and not his valet as expected was priceless.

'Caroline?'

She swept past him and into the room. To her relief, he had the good sense to quickly close the door behind her.

She had rehearsed the next piece in her mind, so had him at a clear disadvantage.

Without a word, she stepped up to him and taking his face in her hands, placed a long seductive kiss on his lips. She sensed his initial hesitation, but when she reached down and lifted up his shirt and took a hold of his manhood she knew she had him at her mercy.

She began to stroke him along the length of his rapidly hardening member.

Ewan broke the kiss.

'Are you sure?'

She nodded. He had wanted a passionate woman in his life, and she was determined to show him that there was fire in her blood.

'I'm not leaving this room a virgin,' she replied.

He puffed out his cheeks. It wasn't every day that a man got that sort of an offer from a woman.

'In that case, I suggest we get some ground rules established. Firstly, that I shall take the lead. Your first time should be special, something on which we can build.'

She swallowed. Nervous at the prospect of finally being with him.

'And secondly, and probably most importantly we are honest with one another. No veils, no secrets. Tonight is where you and I begin, after that only god will separate us.'

He hadn't actually said the words, but she knew in time they would come. She was certain of her path now and no longer feared to set foot on it.

'Yes.'

With careful movements, almost reverent in their gentle grace, Ewan removed Caroline's garments. When he got to the light shift which was the only thing between his hands and her naked form, he stopped.

'I have thought about this moment with you so many times that I lost count. I dreamt of holding you in my bed every night since you arrived. I want you, Caroline. Have no doubt of my need and desire for you.'

With those words, he lifted her shift and she was laid bare to him.

'Beautiful,' he murmured.

He went to his knees before her. When his tongue first touched the slick folds of her womanhood, Caroline sucked in a deep breath.

She closed her eyes and tilted her head back, savoring every moment as he slaved her with his tongue. She had touched herself in bed late at night enough times to know that nothing came close to the pleasure Ewan lavished upon her body.

He rose to his feet before she had reached climax.

'Not yet my sweet. I want to be inside of you when you come.'

He led her over to the bed and sat her down on the edge. His shirt was swiftly removed, giving Caroline her first sight of his naked body.

He caught sight of her looking at his slightly rounded stomach and laughed.

'Too many oatcakes and not enough exercise.'

She leaned forward and placed a tender kiss on his stomach.

'I have read that lovemaking is a wonderful way to get

ne's figure in shape. Consider me your new physician.'

With Ewan standing before her, in his highly aroused
tate, she put all worries aside. Reaching out she took hold
f his manhood once more and ran her tongue along the length
f him.

Ewan sucked in a deep breath.

'Tell me what to do. Teach me how to pleasure you,' she
aid.

'Take me in your mouth, and suck gently,' he whispered.

She did as he instructed, finding that within a short
ime she had a good rhythm established. Ewan speared his
ingers through her hair, guiding her with his hips as to how
eep she should take him. She continued to pleasure him with
er tongue and her mouth for some time before Ewan stopped
er.

'Enough.'

She released him from the pleasure torture she had been
njoying inflicting on him.

He joined her on the bed. He parted the wet folds of her
omanhood and slipped two fingers into her heated body. With
is thumb rubbing the nib of her clitoris, he soon had her on
he cusp of climax once more.

'Ewan,' she pleaded.

He rose over her and took her mouth in a searing kiss.
hen placing his swollen member at her entrance, began to
lowly enter her body.

She felt a twinge, but in an instant, it was gone.

'You are mine now,' he said.

She looked up into his eyes, they were glazed with passion. He was fully in the moment. At the next of his deep strokes, Caroline lay back in the bed and closed her eyes.

Without sight, her senses heightened. With every thrust of Ewan's cock deep into her body, pleasure speared through her. The tension built slowly but steadily. When she felt she was on the verge of reaching the end, he pulled back.

'Not so fast my love. I want this to last until you think you are about to go mad. Then, and only then, will I release you into the depths of your climax.'

She gripped the side of his hips, urging him to come deeply into her once more.

Time and time Ewan held her back. Brought her to the edge of insanity and then held her there.

Finally, even he could not hold back the swelling tide. One final deep thrust into her and Caroline shattered in his arms. Mind altering pleasure coursed through her body.

As the pace of his strokes now increased to a frenzy, Caroline lifted her legs and wrapped them around his hips. Taking him as deep as she could, she pulled him over the edge to join her.

He collapsed on top of her, an exhausted, sated mess.

Later, when she made to leave his bed and head back to her room, fearing discovery from the servants in the morning, wan pulled her close to him. He wrapped his arms around her

nd held in the warmth of the bed.

'This is the bed you sleep in tonight and all nights from

ow on. Go to sleep my love.'

Caroline stole back to her room early Christmas morning, but not until after Ewan had made love to her a second time.

When her maid arrived several hours later, Caroline struggled to get out of bed. She felt twinges in places she didn't know could have twinges.

She dressed in her best gown and retrieved the Christmas gifts she had made from out of her bottom drawer.

Arriving a short time later in the main family sitting room she was greeted with a heart-warming sight.

Ewan was seated by the fire, bouncing David gently on his knee. Next to him on the side of the fireplace hung a branch of Christmas rosemary. On the mantlepiece, an advent wreath had been placed. Around the wreath was wrapped a strip of Strathmore tartan. A lighted candle in the middle of the wreath completed the Christmas decorations.

'You did remember Christmas, thank you' she exclaimed.

She placed her gifts on a nearby table, as Lady Alison and Aunt Maude entered the room.

'Merry Christmas.'

Hugs and Christmas greetings were exchanged all round.

'Now I know you don't celebrate Christmas as such here in Scotland, but I still wanted to give you Christmas gifts. I beg your indulgence. And, I am happy to be here to actually hand them to you,' said Caroline.

The hand knitted scarves were well received by Lady lison and Aunt Maude. They sat as twins on the nearby couch ith their scarves wrapped around necks, matching wide grins n their faces.

Caroline took David in her arms and sat down with him to pen his gift. He barely sniffed at his new clothes, being ore interested in the ribbon on the front of her gown.

There was a knock at the door and Ewan escorted Hannah nto the room.

'Considering Christmas is the season to celebrate the irth of a child, and she was my son's protector from birth I hought it apt that she joins us this morning,' said Ewan.

He took a piece of paper from out of his pocket and anded it to Hannah.

'This is for you, should you choose to accept it.'

Hannah opened the paper and read it for several minutes. hen she looked up she had an worried look on her face.

'It says something about a cottage. And I am not sure hat a stipend is. I don't fully understand what this letter eans your Grace.'

'It means that you will have the run and use of a cottage n the Strathmore estate for the rest of your life. You will lso have a yearly stipend to live on, whether you chose to ake the cottage or not. For all that you have done, I owe you ore than I could ever repay,' he explained.

Hannah looked at Caroline, before bursting into tears.

Ewan had given Hannah freedom from being a servant for the rest of her life. She could choose where and how she would live.

'I believe there is one more gift to come,' said Aunt Maude.

Caroline picked up Ewan's present and handed it to him.

'And this is for you.'

He took the shirt. As he opened the gift and held it up, an awkward silence descended upon the room.

Ewan gave his mother and aunt a sideways look.

'In Scotland, it is customary for only a close female relative, such as a wife to make a man a shirt. Who gave you the idea to make me a shirt?' he said.

Caroline smiled.

'The same people who were so helpful in securing a nursemaid from Edinburgh,' she replied.

The meddling of the Radley women had not gone unnoticed. She has suspected something was afoot after the third of the candidates showed themselves to be unsuitable for the role of David's nursemaid.

It was comforting to know that both Lady Alison and Aunt Maude were keen to see Caroline and Ewan together.

'It's a very thoughtful gift. It shall come to good use. Thank you, Caroline.'

He put down the shirt and held out his hands to take David. As soon as he left Caroline's arms, David began to uss.

'He cannot live without you. And I must confess to being
f the same mind.'

With his son held in his arms, the Duke of Strathmore
ent down on one knee.

David filled his lungs with air and let out a roar. Ewan
ooked down at him in dismay, while Caroline burst into
aughter.

'Whatever it is you are trying to say, I suggest you get
o the point before he gets warmed up to voicing his
isapproval,' she said.

'Marry me. Marry us.'

He pulled a small box from out of his coat pocket and
eld it up.

Caroline took it from his outstretched hand and opened
he box. Inside was a ring. A large ruby with diamonds set
round the outside glistened in the mid-morning sun.

'It has been passed down through the last five Duchesses
f Strathmore. I am hoping with all my heart that you will be
he sixth woman who shall wear it as her betrothal ring.'

She looked from the ring to Ewan who by now was
truggling to stay on his knee and balance the protesting
nfant in his arms.

Hannah stepped forward and took David.

'Sssh, don't fuss my sweet. This is an important moment
n your life,' she murmured to him.

Caroline had played this scene so many times in her mind. Except for the wailing infant, it looked very much like what she had envisioned.

Ewan got to his feet.

Their gazes met.

'As you have no doubt realized by now, I am not possessed of the polish that you would expect from a man of my station. Women have been and still are creatures of mystery to me. What I do know is that over the past weeks one thought has continued to grow stronger in my mind. And in light of events over very recent days, it is the one thing above all others that I need to say to you.'

'Go on.'

He reached out and brushed his hand on her cheek.

'I love you. Will you be my wife, my duchess?'

Their lips met. A tender caress, they both struggled to keep in check.

'I've never stopped loving you. Even after you broke my heart,' she replied.

Ewan pulled the ring from the box and slipped it onto Caroline's finger.

'I will never hurt you again. From this day forth I am yours if you will have me.'

'Yes.'

CHAPTER TWENTY-SEVEN

When Ewan said from this day forth, Caroline thought he meant their betrothal. What she soon realized was that he intended for her to be the Duchess of Strathmore from this very day.

Unbeknownst to her, the castle had been a hive of prewedding activity from early light. The family chapel was hastily decorated with whatever flowers or pretty herbs which could be found. The village minister had been summoned from his bed and made ready for the wedding party in his best robes.

The courtyard had been swept clear of snow and a second bonfire constructed. Barrels of ale and whisky had been tapped in readiness for the wedding feast. Freshly caught boars were roasting on the spits. The castle cook had staff hurrying back and forth from the kitchens to the dry food stores.

All the castle staff and the nearby villagers were gathered inside the castle walls. It was not every day that the Duke of Strathmore got married and no one was going to miss the celebrations.

All that was required now was the bride.

Caroline dressed in a cream gown, with a Strathmore tartan sash draped from her shoulder walked the short distance from the castle keep to the chapel. In her hair, she wore the Hastings family gold and pearl tiara.

Lady Alison and Aunt Maude sat in the front row of the chapel, alongside them were David and his newly appointed nursemaid Hannah. With her sweetheart still in the navy, she had made the generous offer to stay with the Radley family until she was able to marry and bring her new husband to live in the cottage gifted to her on the Strathmore estate.

Both Ewan and Caroline thoroughly approved of the choice of nursemaid.

Caroline's heart swelled with emotion when Ewan, standing in front of the altar turned and smiled at her. Under his black velvet coat and breeches, he wore a Strathmore tartan waistcoat. Under the waistcoat, he proudly wore the white shirt his new bride had made for him.

As she reached his side, he turned and gave her a tender kiss on the lips. The minister looked down at his Bible and pretended he had not seen anything.

'I love you, Caroline Hastings. I couldn't be happier knowing that you are to be by my side for the rest of my life.'

'I love you too.'

She had never thought to be a Christmas Day bride, but of
ll the gifts she could have wished for, knowing that the man
he was about to marry truly loved her was the most precious
ift of all.

Her Scottish duke was finally hers.

EPILOGUE

'Hush now my lad.'

Caroline kissed the forehead of the newborn she held in her arms, as she tried to settle him.

'He has the same set of lungs as his brother,' Ewan said.

He reached down and picked up a squirming David, who was now a strapping toddler. David was excited to see the new baby.

'Baby Alex,' said David.

The Duke and Duchess of Strathmore exchanged a smile. The first of David's siblings had finally arrived. A child conceived in love and welcomed in the second year of their marriage.

Alex Radley, Marquess of Brooke.

More Duke of Strathmore Books

Read Alex, David and their sister Lucy's stories.

Alex Radley - Letter from a Rake

David Radley - An Unsuitable Match

Lucy Radley - The Duke's Daughter

Made in the USA
Monee, IL
07 November 2019